Feb 15, 2016

MW00979052

Hope you find
joy in your
Hobby :)

xo:
Lisa S.

Bow Ties of Bravery Alphabet Series

Brought to you by Lise Steeves
Of
Lises' Library

Bow Ties of Bravery Alphabet Series

Dedication

The Bow Ties of Bravery Series is dedicated for those of you
looking for something a little different.

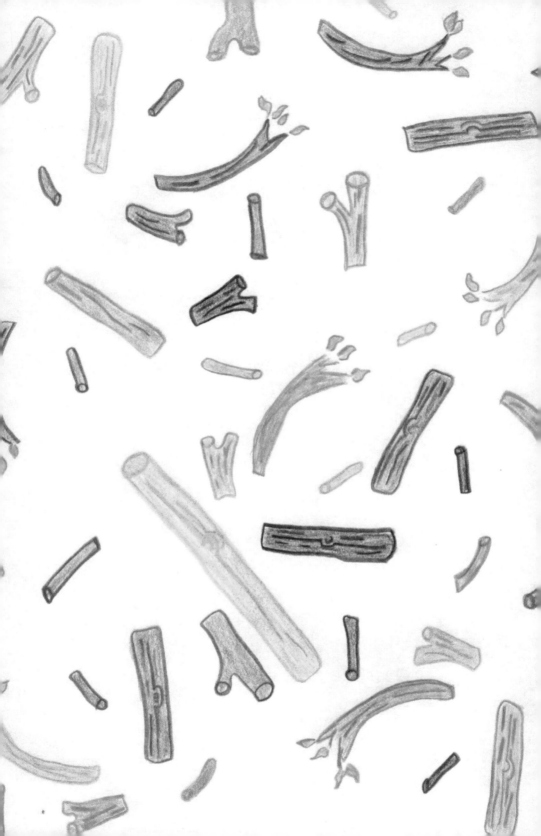

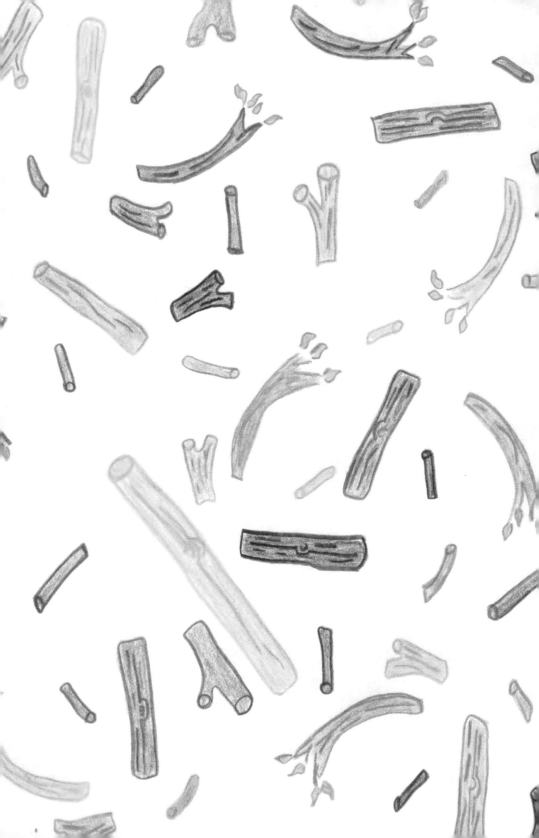

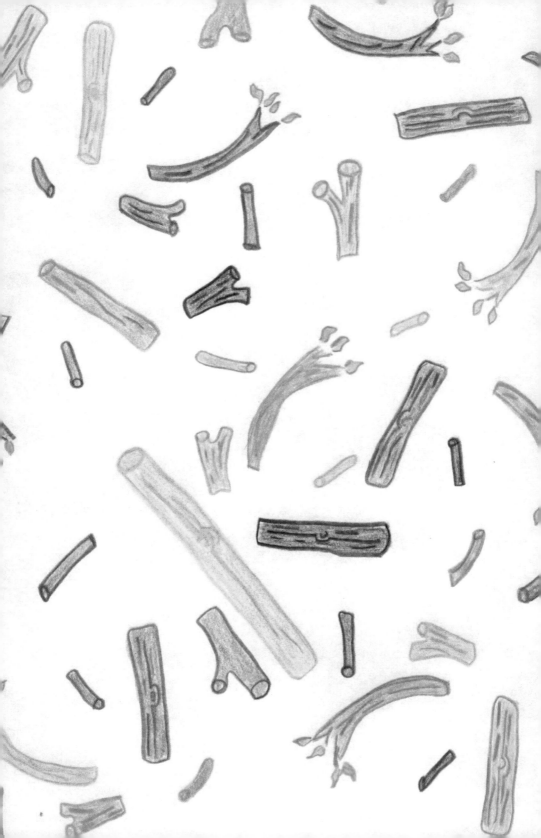

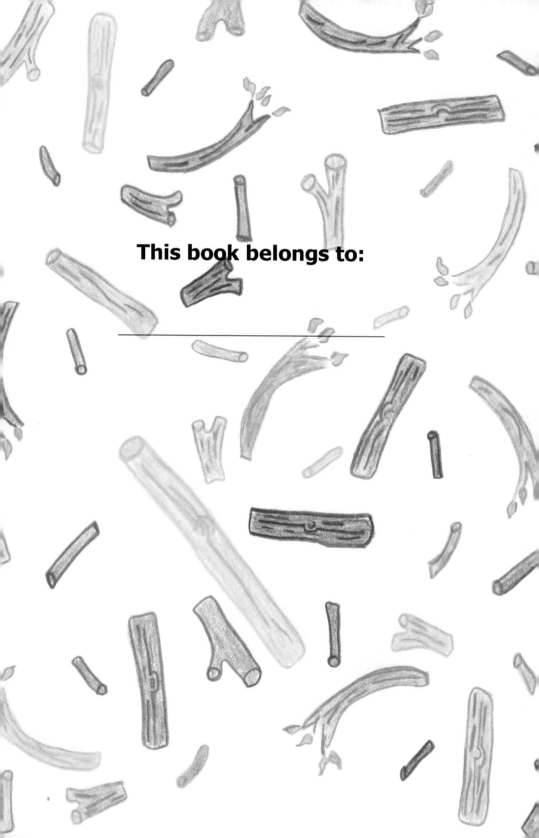

This book belongs to:

_____

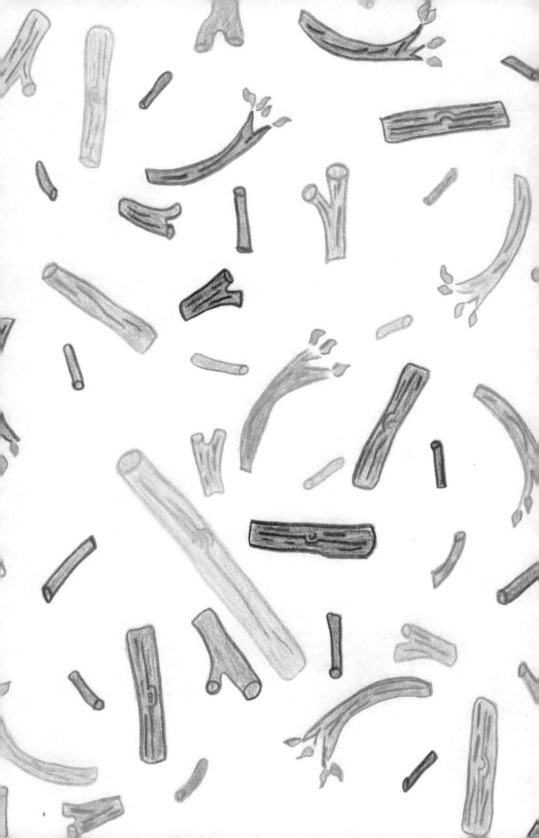

Berry
The Beaver

Is a Builder

Berry the Beaver lived in the Canadian Bush with his family, Mamma Beaver, Poppa Beaver, Brother Ben, and Sister Betty.

Momma Beaver and Poppa Beaver would
encourage their little Beavers to go out and discover
the world.
Berry, Ben, and Betty all found hobbies they enjoyed.

Brother Ben likes to lift Bar Bells.

Sister Betty likes to Meditate on the Beach.

Berry likes to Build Bird Houses.

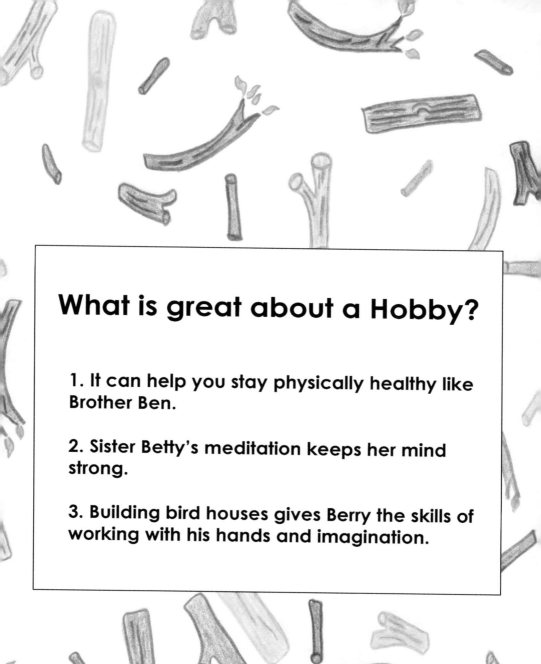

What is great about a Hobby?

1. It can help you stay physically healthy like Brother Ben.

2. Sister Betty's meditation keeps her mind strong.

3. Building bird houses gives Berry the skills of working with his hands and imagination.

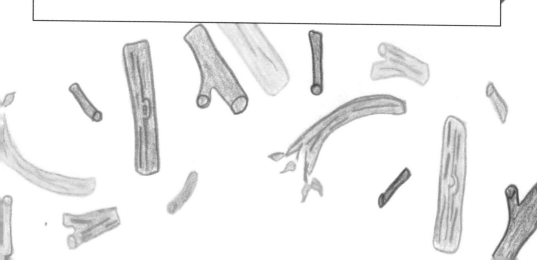

Momma and Poppa Beaver were so very proud of their little Beavers.
The house they were living in was getting pretty crowded with everyone growing up so fast.
Berry talked to Momma and Poppa Beaver and they decided that Berry had grown up so big and strong, that it was time for him to move out on his own.

Momma Beaver fixed Berry's Bravery Bow Tie one last time.
So excited, Berry said good bye to his family, and headed
out to build a life of his own.

Berry the Beaver thought about his favorite places that would be great for his first home.
He walked up to his hobby tree and saw it was surrounded with beautiful bushes.
"I'm home!" said Berry.

Beau the bird came by to see how Berry was making out in his new home.

"This will be perfect!" Berry joyfully announced to his friend.
"You know...all the Beaver houses are built the same but mine is different!" Berry exclaimed with his hands on his hips and nose in the air.

"Berry, it's great to build differently, but don't you think there is a reason beavers build the way they do?" Beau asked.
Beau was trying to be supportive of his friend, but a little worried Berry hadn't thought his home choice through.

"You know, I wanted to live at the North Pole, but it was problematic for me being a little bird." Beau said with disappointment.
"But I made a great nest here and am very happy!"

Berry brushed his friends concerns aside and settled in for the night.

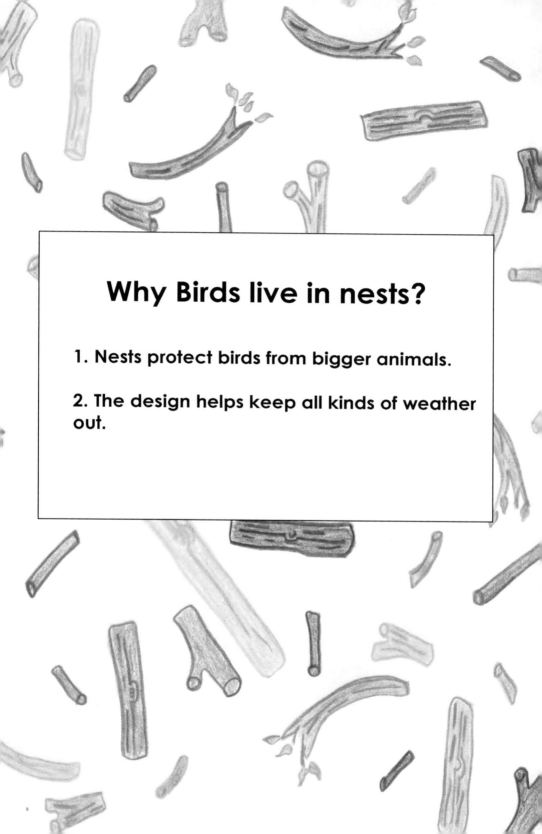

Why Birds live in nests?

1. Nests protect birds from bigger animals.

2. The design helps keep all kinds of weather out.

There was a strange noise coming from the bush house.
Berry popped his head out to see the wind was

BLOOOOWWWWING

on the bush house leaves, making them rustle.
He ducked down into the bush house and got a shiver
from the biting wind blowing through the walls.

Burrrrrr!

Berry's teeth started to chatter.

A short time later Berry felt a

DRIP

DRIP

DRIP

on his head.

It had started to rain.
Berry was now cold, wet, and could not sleep.

When morning came, Berry was sad that his bush house
had not worked out.
He felt as though he had failed.
Sister Betty came by to check on Berry after his first night
on his own.

"How are you?" she inquired with anticipation of a fabulous
story of what it's like to have your own home.

"Not so well." Berry was embarrassed to say.

"What happened?" she asked nervously.

Berry told her of the wind

BLOOOOWWWWING

in and how the rain

DR↓P

DR↓P

DR↓PPED

on his head all night long.

"Oh my!" replied Sister Betty. "Hey, why don't you build a Beaver Dam House like Momma and Poppa Beaver have? I'll help you!" offered Sister Betty.

"Oh, no, no", said Berry, "I'm a Big, Strong and Brilliant Beaver. I can do it myself. Besides, I want it to be different than all the other Beaver Houses!"

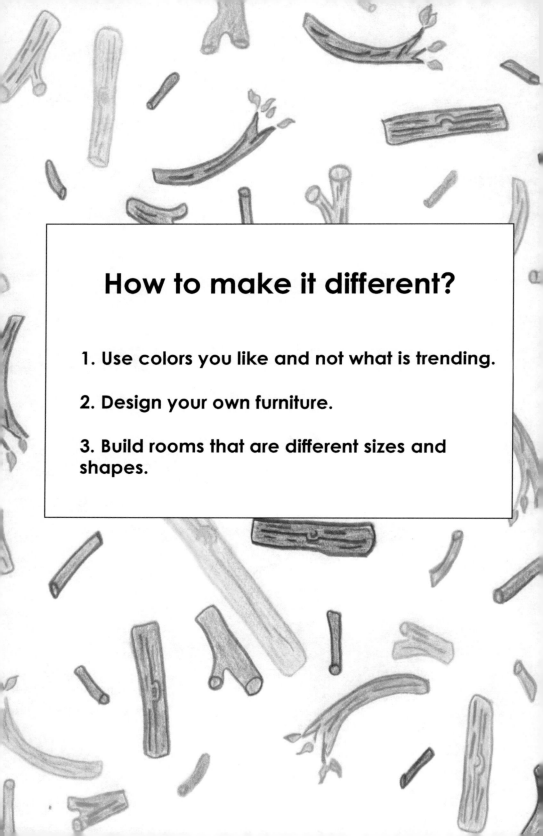

How to make it different?

1. Use colors you like and not what is trending.

2. Design your own furniture.

3. Build rooms that are different sizes and shapes.

Berry moving out and making it through a tough night inspired Sister Betty and Brother Ben to move out also. Sister Betty and Brother Ben wanted to be sure they were making the right choices, so they asked the family for help.

Berry laughed at them and said "My first house may not have been so great, but I built my Beaver House all by myself."

When the family was finished building Sister Betty and Brother Ben's houses, Poppa Beaver said "Now, to know that it is built properly, we need to do the Beaver Builders Test".

The family stood atop of Sister Betty's house, and it did not cave in.

"Great job!" Momma Beaver said with pride.

They all moved on to Brother Ben's house for the Beaver Builder Test, and it stood up strong.

"Very nice job everyone!" said Poppa Beaver with a big smile.

"Well, that's great!" Berry congratulated his brother and sister.
"But I built my house on my own, so go ahead and try your test on it." Berry scoffed with his nose in the air.

"Sure!" said Brother Ben.

The family climbed atop of Berry's house.
All of a sudden there was cracking and creaking noises.

The family disappeared in a cloud of dust.

"BERRY'S HOUSE CAVED IN!" Sister Betty screamed.

"Is everyone alright?" Momma asked as they all climbed out of the big hole.

Berry was relieved everyone was okay.
He felt bad that he had stuck his nose in the air, and bragged he
built his home himself.
Like his first home, he had a sense of failure because his house
did not work out.
Poppa Beaver told Berry he was very proud of him for trying to
build his homes on his own.
Berry was surprised Poppa Beaver was not upset with him for his
bad behavior.

"Sometimes, no matter how Big, Strong, and Brilliant a Beaver
may be, it is a good idea to ask for help." Poppa Beaver wisely
explained.

"Yes Poppa", Berry cried, "I'm so sorry!"

Wiping his tears away, Berry asked the family for their help
building his dream Beaver House.

The family understood that Berry's pride got the best of him, and he had learned from his snobbery.
They helped him build the most unique Beaver House in all of the Canadian Bush.

Berry's house also passed the Beavers Builder Test.

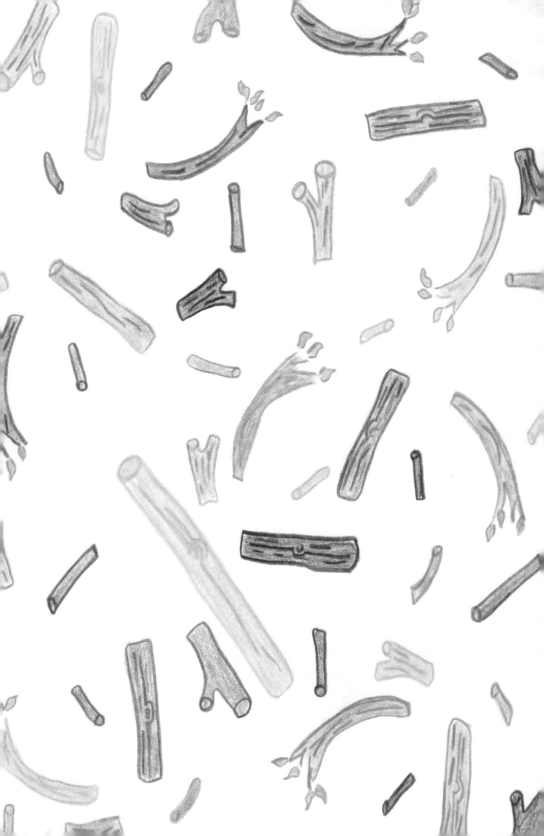

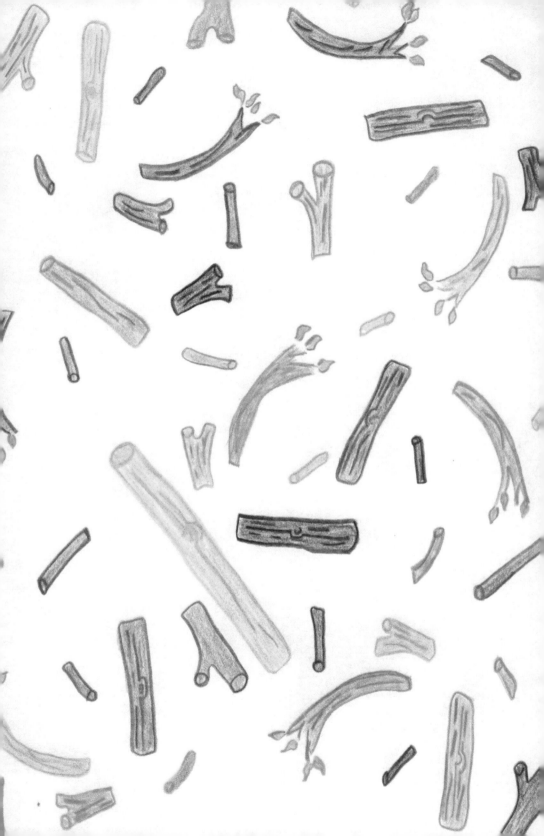

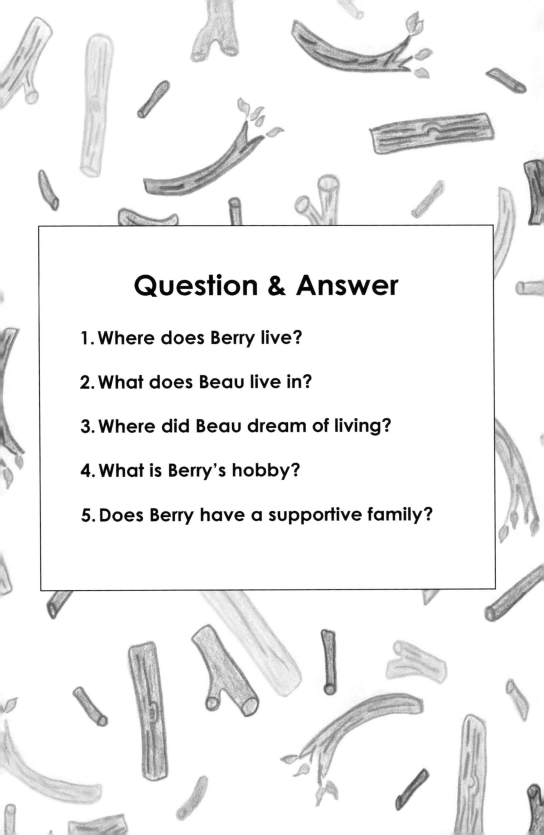

Question & Answer

1. Where does Berry live?

2. What does Beau live in?

3. Where did Beau dream of living?

4. What is Berry's hobby?

5. Does Berry have a supportive family?

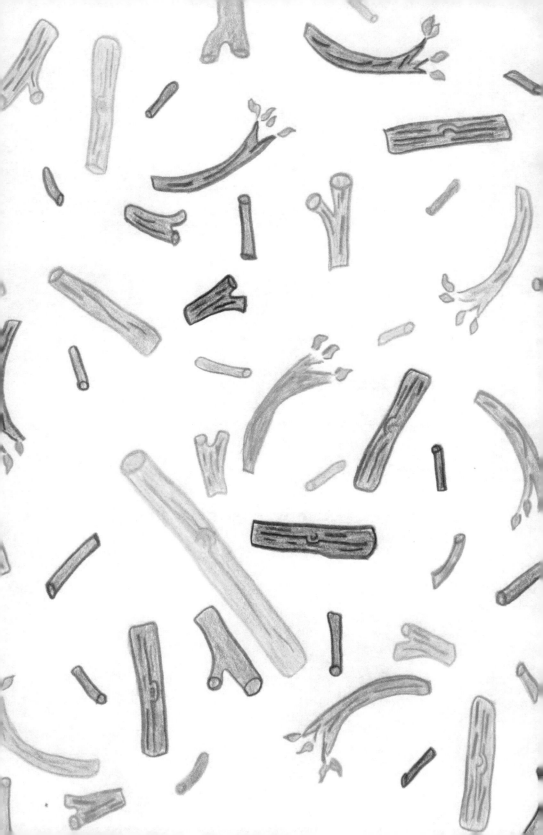

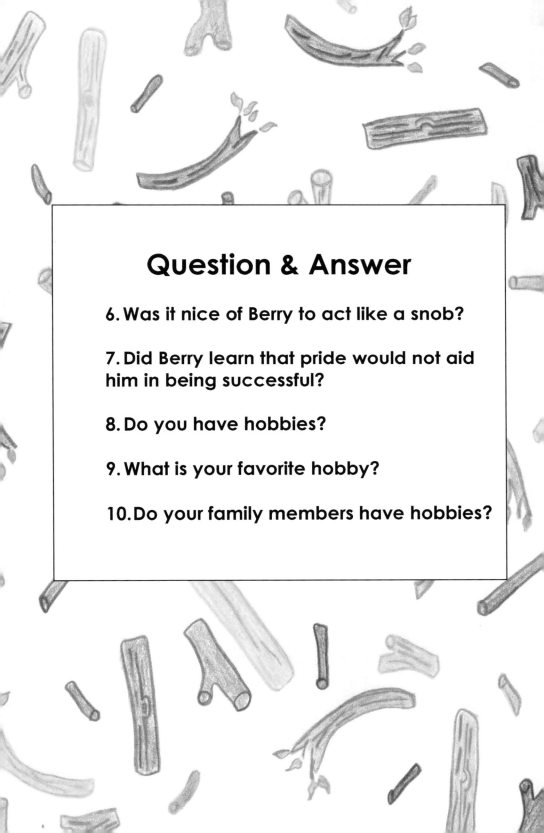

Question & Answer

6. Was it nice of Berry to act like a snob?

7. Did Berry learn that pride would not aid him in being successful?

8. Do you have hobbies?

9. What is your favorite hobby?

10. Do your family members have hobbies?

Lise Steeves is a published writer. Miss Steeves' first publication came out in the late 1980's with her letter "To the Unknown Soldier" through St. Benedict Catholic School. Writing has always been a dream of hers and she is happy to bring it to you now under "Lises' Library", the "Bow Ties of Bravery Alphabet Series."

The Bow Tie of Bravery is there for all of us in good times and bad. Whether it is visible or imaginary, it is there to help give us grace, strength, and courage as we face life while we grow.

Next in line for the

Bow Ties of Bravery
Alphabet Series

By Lises' Library

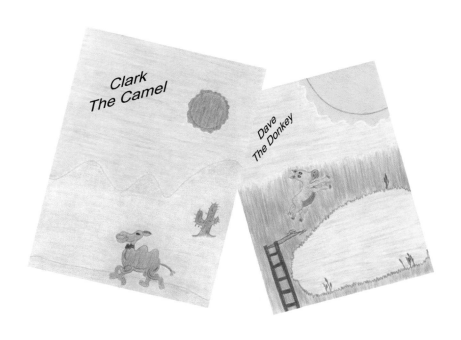

Made in the USA
Charleston, SC
05 February 2016